FOR JANET LILY SISLOWITZ
J. Y.

FOR MY FRIEND, ABBY
D. A.

SIMON AND SCHUSTER
First published in Great Britain in 2016 by Simon and Schuster UK Ltd
1st Floor, 222 Gray's Inn Road, London, WC1X 8HB
A CBS Company

Originally published in 2012 by Simon & Schuster Books for Young Readers,
an imprint of Simon and Schuster Children's Publishing Division, New York

A CIP catalogue record for this book is available from the British Library upon request

978-1-4711-6041-7 (PB)

WAKING DRAGONS

by JANE YOLEN

PAINTINGS BY DEREK ANDERSON

SIMON AND SCHUSTER

London   New York   Sydney   Toronto   New Delhi

Dragons wake up,

dragons rise.

Dragons open
dragon eyes.

Dragons blink,
dragons bumble,

dragons leap,
dragons tumble
out of bed

to brush their teeth,
the fangs above,
the fangs beneath.

Put their jammies
in the hamper.

Then all dragons
skip and scamper

down the hall
on four big feet
to the kitchen
there to eat

breakfast waffles,
topped with syrup,
which makes dragons
really cheer up.

Wipe their faces,
runny noses,

get into their
outdoor clothes-es.

Kiss their dragon
mum goodbye.
Leap from cave
into the sky,

where dragons
get to fly.

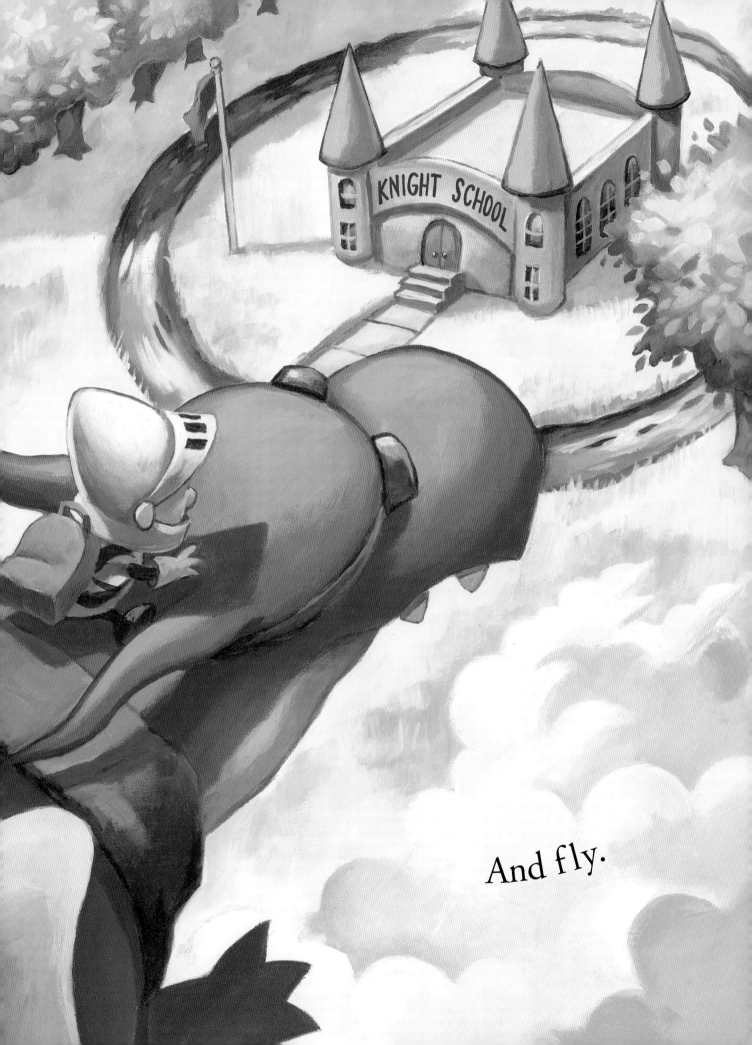

And fly.

And fly.